MW01042102

Funny Bone Readers™

Truck Pals on the Job

Gus and the Mighty Mess

written and illustrated by Ken Bowser

RED
CHAIR
•PRESS•™

Funny Bone Readers and Funny Bone Books are published by Red Chair Press
Red Chair Press LLC   PO Box 333   South Egremont, MA 01258-0333
www.redchairpress.com

For my Grandson, Liam Hayden Bowser
who never met a truck he didn't like.

Publisher's Cataloging-In-Publication Data
Bowser, Ken.

  Gus and the mighty mess / written and illustrated by Ken Bowser.

   pages : illustrations ; cm. -- (Funny bone readers. Truck pals on the job)

  Summary: Garbage trucks are supposed to keep our neighborhoods clean and tidy. But
when Gus loses trash by accident, he must call on friends to help him clean up the mess.

  Interest age level: 004-008.

  ISBN: 978-1-63440-065-7 (library hardcover)

  ISBN: 978-1-63440-066-4 (paperback)

  Issued also as an ebook. (ISBN: 978-1-63440-067-1)

  1. Refuse collection vehicles--Juvenile fiction. 2. Teams in the workplace--Juvenile
fiction. 3. Friendship--Juvenile fiction. 4. Refuse collection vehicles--Fiction. 5. Teams in
the workplace--Fiction. 6. Friendship--Fiction. I. Title.

PZ7.B697 Gu 2016

[E]   2015938000

Printed in the United States of America
Distributed in the U.S. by Lerner Publisher Services. www.lernerbooks.com

1015 1P WRZSP16

Gus was a giant, purple garbage truck.
He worked hard every day.
Working hard made him very happy.

His strong arms could lift big, heavy
cans and empty them into the back
of his great, big truck bed.

4

At the end of a long day, his truck was always full! It made Gus happy to do a good job.

But today was not just any day. Gus was not paying attention. A big rock became stuck in the back of his heavy tailgate.

Gus did not see that his tailgate was stuck open by the rock. "Done for the day!" Gus said. And off he went!

As Gus drove away, something very
bad was happening. Trash was blowing
out from his tailgate!

Papers and bits of trash were spilling
out everywhere! Oh this was NOT
good! This was NOT good at ALL!

Gus could see the messy scene behind him from his rear view mirror. "Oh no! I'm leaving a gigantic mess," he groaned.

Now there were pieces of trash on the
street as far as Gus could see. "I am in
very BIG trouble NOW!" Gus worried.

Gus tried hard for a long time to
pick up all of the trash and paper.
"My arms are strong," he thought.
"But I just can't pick up these little pieces."

He kept trying his hardest. He picked
up a few things but his arms could not
reach the back of the truck! "I just can't
do this alone," he said.

Gus asked School Bus for help. "I'm sorry, Gus. I'm just for carrying boys and girls," she told him.

Dump Truck stopped too. "I'm not built for that," he said. "I'm made for hauling big, heavy loads."

Ice Cream Truck came by. "Gosh Gus," she said. "I'm just made for keeping things cold."

"We're so sorry, Gus," they said. "That's okay. I understand," Gus told them as they drove away.

Gus looked at the messy street. "What can I do? I've tried my best. I've asked my friends. I think I'm in big trouble!"

It was getting late. Gus was worried.
He felt sad about the mess he made.
He had not done a good job today.

Then, Gus heard strange sounds that he had not heard before. They were odd, scary sounds. "Whir, whir! Whoosh, whoosh! Scrubba, scrubba!"

18

The sounds grew louder and
louder. "WHIR, WHIR! WHOOOSH,
WHOOOSH! SCRUBBA, SCRUBBA"!
"What is that noise?" Gus wondered.

Now Gus saw where the sounds were coming from. "What strange truck are you?" Gus asked. "I'm Street Sweeper Sam! Your friends said you needed help!"

Sam went to work right away and
began to sweep up all of the bits of
paper and trash! "I can't lift big things,"
said Sam. "But I can tidy up!"

Gus and Sam looked out over the clean
streets. Gus was thankful for his friends
and Sam was proud that he could help.

Everything turned out fine and Gus
headed home after a long day's work.

Big Questions: Do you think Gus was trying to make a mess for fun? Who came to help Gus clean the streets? Think of two words to describe Gus.

Big Words:

garbage: trash, items thrown away

tailgate: a flap or door at the back of a truck that can be moved to load or unload the truck